SECRET AGENT

The Fight for the Frozen Land:
ARCTIC

BOOK (12)

D0089887

Join Secret Agent Jack Stalwart on his other adventures:

The Escape of the Deadly Dinosaur:
USA
Book ①

The Search for the Sunken Treasure:
AUSTRALIA
Book ②

The Mystery of the Mona Lisa:
FRANCE
Book ③

The Caper of the Crown Jewels:
ENGLAND
Book ④

The Secret of the Sacred Temple:
CAMBODIA
Book ⑤

The Pursuit of the Ivory Poachers:
KENYA
Book ⑥

The Puzzle of the Missing Panda:
CHINA
Book ⑦

Peril at the Grand Prix:
ITALY
Book ⑧

The Deadly Race to Space:
RUSSIA
Book ⑨

The Quest for Aztec Gold:
MEXICO
Book ⑩

The Theft of the Samurai Sword:
JAPAN
Book ⑪

The Fight for the Frozen Land:
ARCTIC

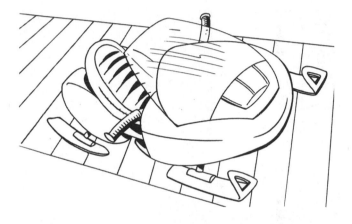

Elizabeth Singer Hunt

Illustrated by Brian Williamson

WEINSTEIN BOOKS

*For everyone working furiously to halt
climate change*

THE ARCTIC CIRCLE

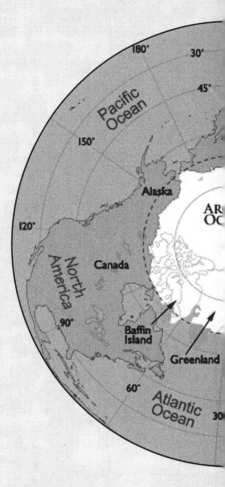

Destination:
ARCTIC

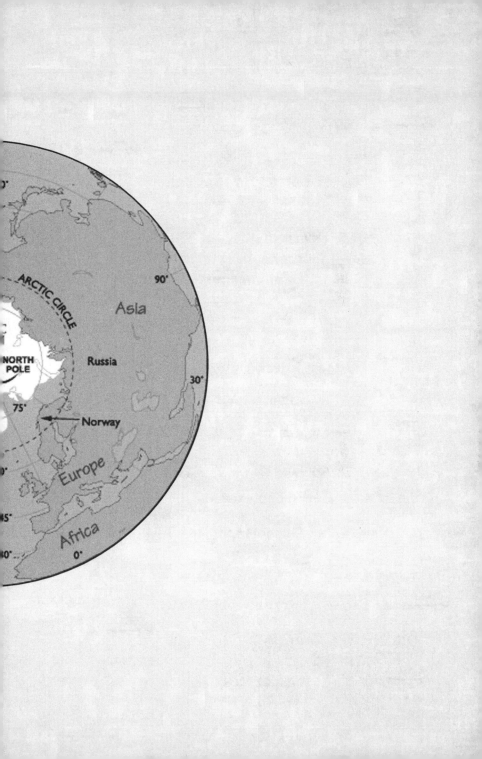

Jack Stalwart applied to be a secret
agent for the Global Protection
Force four months ago.

My name is Jack Stalwart. My older brother,
Max, was a secret agent for you, until he
disappeared on one of your missions. Now I
want to be a secret agent too. If you choose
me, I will be an excellent secret agent and get
rid of evil villains, just like my brother did.

Sincerely,

Jack Stalwart

Jack Stalwart was sworn in as a Global
Protection Force secret agent four months ago.
Since that time, he has completed all of his
missions successfully and has stopped no less
than twelve evil villains. Because of this he
has been assigned the code name "COURAGE."

Jack has yet to uncover the whereabouts of
his brother, Max, who is still working for this
organization at a secret location. Do not give
Secret Agent Jack Stalwart this information.
He is never to know about his brother.

Gerald Barter

Gerald Barter
Director, Global Protection Force

THINGS YOU'LL FIND IN EVERY BOOK

 **Watch Phone:** The only gadget Jack wears all the time, even when he's not on official business. His Watch Phone is the central gadget that makes most others work. There are lots of important features, most importantly the "C" button, which reveals the code of the day—necessary to unlock Jack's Secret Agent Book Bag. There are buttons on both sides, one of which ejects his life-saving Melting Ink Pen. Beyond these functions, it also works as a phone and, of course, gives Jack the time of day.

 **Global Protection Force (GPF):** The GPF is the organization Jack works for. It's a worldwide force of young secret agents whose aim is to protect the world's people, places and possessions. No one knows exactly where its main offices are located (all correspondence and gadgets for repair are sent to a special P.O. Box, and training is held at various locations around the world), but Jack thinks it's somewhere cold, like the Arctic Circle.

Whizzy: Jack's magical miniature globe. Almost every night at precisely 7:30 P.M., the GPF uses Whizzy to send Jack the identity of the country that he must travel to. Whizzy can't talk, but he can cough up messages. Jack's parents don't know Whizzy is anything more than a normal globe.

The Magic Map: The magical map hanging on Jack's bedroom wall. Unlike most maps, the GPF's map is made of a mysterious wood. Once Jack inserts the country piece from Whizzy, the map swallows Jack whole and sends him away on his missions. When he returns, he arrives precisely one minute after he left.

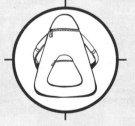

Secret Agent Book Bag: The Book Bag that Jack wears on every adventure. Licensed only to GPF secret agents, it contains top-secret gadgets necessary to foil bad guys and escape certain death. To activate the bag before each mission, Jack must punch in a secret code given to him by his Watch Phone. Once he's away, all he has to do is place his finger on the zip, which identifies him as the owner of the bag and immediately opens.

THE STALWART FAMILY

Jack's dad, John

He moved the family to England when Jack was two, in order to take a job with an aerospace company. Jack's dad thinks he is an ordinary boy and that his other son, Max, attends a school in Switzerland. Jack's dad is American and his mum is British, which makes Jack a bit of both.

Jack's mum, Corinne

One of the greatest mums as far as Jack is concerned. When she and her husband received a letter from a posh school in Switzerland inviting Max to attend, they were overjoyed. Since Max left six months ago, they have received numerous notes in Max's handwriting telling them he's OK. Little do they know it's all a lie and that it's the GPF sending those letters.

Jack's older brother, Max

Two years ago, at the age of nine, Max joined the GPF. Max used to tell Jack about his adventures and show him how to work his secret-agent gadgets. When the family received a letter inviting Max to attend a school in Europe, Jack figured it was to do with the GPF. Max told him he was right, but that he couldn't tell Jack anything about why he was going away.

Nine-year-old Jack Stalwart

Four months ago, Jack received an anonymous note saying: "Your brother is in danger. Only you can save him." As soon as he could, Jack applied to be a secret agent too. Since that time, he's battled some of the world's most dangerous villains, and hopes some day in his travels to find and rescue his brother, Max.

DESTINATION:
Arctic

The Arctic includes the northern parts of eight countries: Canada, Greenland, Russia, Alaska, Iceland, Norway, Sweden and Finland.

□

The word "Arctic" comes from the Greek word "Arktos," or "bear."

□

The Arctic isn't actually a country, but an area of land, ice and water north of the Arctic Circle.

□

Temperatures in the Arctic can range from around 45°F in the summer to minus 29°F in the winter.

□

Polar bears, seals, walruses, beluga whales, narwhal whales, reindeer, arctic foxes and wolves live in the Arctic.

GPF ANIMAL FACTS: THE POLAR BEAR

The polar bear is the world's largest land predator.

They are thought to have evolved from brown bears about 200,000 years ago, developing jagged teeth, large feet, a longer nose and short claws to hunt and survive in the extreme Arctic conditions.

Rising global temperatures is causing sea ice to melt. Although polar bears are excellent swimmers, they now have to travel further to find food.

Polar bears are listed as an "endangered species."

GPF FAST FACTS: GLOBAL WARMING

Global warming means that our planet's overall temperature is rising—by as much as 6.4 degrees in the next hundred years.

Greenhouse gases trap heat into our atmosphere, keeping us warm.
But levels of these gases, especially carbon dioxide, have recently risen to dangerous levels.

Many species will become extinct, and weather will become more extreme.

If we want to stop global warming from getting worse, we all have to work together as a team.

GPF GUIDE TO SAVING THE PLANET

Here's what you can do to help keep our planet cool:

Turn the lights off when you leave a room.

Use less water by turning the tap off while you brush your teeth.

Encourage your family to bike and walk places instead of using the car.

Recycle plastic and glass bottles, aluminium cans, cardboard and paper.

Plant a tree somewhere—trees take in carbon dioxide and give off oxygen instead.

SECRET AGENT GADGET INSTRUCTION MANUAL

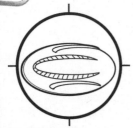

Sno-Sled: When you need to slide down a hill or pick up speed on a slick surface, use the GPF's Sno-Sled. Just pull out this oval-shaped plastic board, get a running start and sit on the middle. Make sure to hold onto the handles, as the Sno-Sled can travel at speeds of up to 80 mph.

Poison Tracker: When you need to analyze a mystery dust or liquid, use the GPF's Poison Tracker Kit. Use the gloves and the spoon to pick up the substance and place it into one of the glass vials. Within seconds the side of the vial will change color. Red means deadly; yellow is dangerous; and green is OK.

Sno-Speed: The GPF's Sno-Speed is the most technologically advanced and environmentally friendly snowmobile in the world. It travels over ice and snow at speeds of up to 200 mph, and uses a hydrogen fuel cell to make it go. It is equipped with a satellite navigation system, spotlights and a jagged knife on the side. Most impressive, it works by mind control. Just ask it to come, and it will find you.

Polar Parka: When you're working in freezing conditions, make sure you have your GPF Polar Parka. The Polar Parka is made of a special material that reacts to cold temperatures to keep your body comfortably warm. It has a glow-in-the-dark feature that enables others to find you if you're stranded or in trouble.

Chapter 1:
The Frozen Land

It was an early spring morning in the Arctic. Three scientists (two men and one woman) were standing over a table inside their warming hut. They were reviewing their map and preparing for the day's work. This was day number twenty-eight in their month-long assignment. Only a few more outings and they'd be ready to publish their findings.

"Let's take measurements from here

today," said the woman, pointing to a spot fifty miles away. "No one has collected data from this area before."

"Good idea," said another scientist. "It will be good to compare the thickness of the ice there with other locations."

The scientists pulled on their snowsuits and strapped on their boots. Stepping outside, they looked at the thermometer hanging by the door of the hut. The mercury read 20°F.

"Another warm day in one of the coldest places on Earth," said one. The other scientists chuckled at the joke.

After fastening their tools to their snowmobiles, they started the engines. Within moments, the trio was traveling across the frozen plain.

Within an hour, they'd arrived at their destination. They hopped off their snowmobiles and began organizing their tools. One of the scientists noticed some buildings in the distance. They looked like isolated warming huts.

"What are they?" said one.

"Let's check them out," said another.

As they walked toward the huts an enormous noise ripped through the air.

KABOOM!

Behind the buildings, chunks of ice and earth burst from the ground. The force of the explosion was so great, it knocked the trio off their feet.

Dazed, the scientists lay on their backs.
Soon they were aware of another sound.
This time it was the roaring sound of
approaching snowmobiles, getting closer
and closer.

BRRRM!

BRRRM!

"Who do you think that is?" said one of
the men, looking scared.

"I don't know," said the woman.

The drivers of the snowmobiles had black helmets painted with flames and darkened visors covering their eyes.

"I have a bad feeling about this," said the other man.

"Me too," said the woman. "Let's get out of here."

The scientists crawled to their knees and began to run. They sprinted in the direction of their snowmobiles. If they

could get to a radio, they could call for help.

SWOOSH!

The first snowmobile slid in front, blocking their path. The scientists turned and ran the other way.

SWOOSH!

The second snowmobile trapped them from behind. Realizing what was happening, the trio looked around wildly.

"Don't hurt us," said one scientist. He put his hands in the air to show he didn't have any weapons.

"We won't tell anyone what we've seen," pleaded the woman. By now all of the scientists had their hands held high.

"We know you won't," sniggered one of the drivers. Pulling a long tube from his rucksack, he flashed it at the scientists.

"Please don't!" begged one of the men. Although he didn't know what the tube was for, he had a feeling it wouldn't be good news.

But the driver ignored their pleas. He aimed the tube at the scientists, and pumped the lever that was underneath. A fine dust burst into their faces. As it crept into their noses, they fell to the ground with a thud.

"Let's tie them up," said one driver to the other. "And kill their radios."

The drivers smashed the scientists' communication equipment. Then they tied them to the back of their snowmobiles. After congratulating each other on a job well done, the drivers left the area with the scientists' dazed bodies trailing behind.

Chapter 2:
The Warming Planet

Around the same time, but in a very different part of the world, Jack Stalwart was sitting at his desk, doing his homework. He'd been asked by his geography teacher, Mrs. Corry, to prepare a presentation on global warming. She wanted him to show that it existed, say what caused it and what, if anything, their class could do to help.

Jack knew that for many of his fellow

students the idea that the planet was warming up was a hard one to swallow. After all, England had just finished its coldest winter yet. Last spring there was snow on the ground at Easter! And last summer was one of the most pleasantly mild on record. But even though things at home seemed fine at the moment, global warming was causing wacky weather events elsewhere.

The southern states of America had just been battered by one of the worst hurricanes on record. In Europe, summer temperatures soared to 104°F (40°C) over a two week period. Last spring, a devastating cyclone hit Southeast Asia killing more than a hundred thousand people. And the scientific station in Antarctica recently reported that the Wilkins Ice Shelf—one of the continent's biggest—was about to crack and fall off into the sea due to melting.

Jack knew all of this thanks to the GPF. Jack was an agent for the Global Protection Force, or GPF; the only organization of young secret agents created to help protect the world. Rescuing an important person, a precious monument or priceless work of art were all examples of the kinds of things a GPF secret agent did.

For years the GPF had been working behind the scenes on global warming research. They were among the first to show that increases in carbon dioxide led to increases in global temperatures. In fact, the GPF had just sent out a team of scientists to research the effects of global warming on the Arctic. Jack had received a classified note about it via the secure GPF website.

Proving to his class that the planet was changing wasn't going to be difficult. He just needed to organize his facts and write them down. With that, he signed onto his computer, pulled up a blank document, and began to type out his report.

Chapter 3:
The White Card

Just then, Jack's Watch Phone began to beep. It was almost 7:30P.M.—the time of day when the GPF sent Jack the location of his next mission.

After saving his document, Jack shut the lid on his laptop. He walked over to his bedside table and looked at Whizzy, his miniature globe, who was just waking up. Whizzy opened his eyes, winked at Jack, and began spinning furiously in a clockwise direction. Jack was definitely off on a mission tonight!

When Whizzy was ready, he coughed— "Ahem!"—and a jigsaw piece flew out of his mouth. It skimmed the top of Jack's duvet and glided like a model airplane across the room. When it landed smoothly on the floor, Jack rushed over to it. But when he got there, he was a bit confused.

Normally, when Whizzy spat something out, it was a jigsaw piece in the shape of a country. Jack would then take the piece to the Magic Map on his wall. When he matched it to the correct spot, the map would swallow him up and transport him to a new place.

But this piece wasn't in the shape of any country. In fact, it was just a small white rectangular card with a number code written on it. This could only mean one thing. The GPF's director, Gerald Barter, wanted to speak to Jack in person.

As he walked over to the map with the card, Jack's heart started to thump. He wondered why he was being summoned. Agents NEVER got to meet Gerald Barter in person unless they or someone else was in serious trouble.

The GPF had worked hard over the years to keep its true headquarter's location a secret, even from its own GPF agents. Agent training in gadgetry, martial arts and other areas had been held at top secret locations around the world. When an agent needed to repair a gadget, they had to send it via secure post to an anonymous P.O. Box. And when the GPF had to announce something to the press, it was always a one-way message with reporters unable to ask direct questions to the organization.

Jack had always figured it was somewhere cold and remote, but he

didn't have any hard evidence. As he
placed the rectangular card in a slot at
the bottom right corner of the map, he
took a deep breath. He was finally about
to find out.

Chapter 4:
The Blinking Lights

As soon as Jack placed the card into a
space in the bottom right hand corner of
the map, lights began to appear all over—
first in Europe, then in Africa, then in
South America. Usually, a single light
appeared confirming the location of his
next adventure. But this time, the lights
were all over the place. The GPF wasn't
going to reveal the location of its
headquarters to Jack just yet.

Jack rushed over to his bed and grabbed his Book Bag from underneath. He checked his Watch Phone for the code of the day, keying it into his Book Bag's lock. The code word P-L-A-N-E-T didn't give Jack any clues either.

Looking inside, Jack checked his gadgets. There were the usual gadgets, like the Net Tosser, Noggin Mold and Poison Tracker. The presence of the Sno-Sled gave Jack a small hint of where it might be.

He rushed back to the Magic Map, strapping his Book Bag on tight. He waited as the lights on the map lit up at the same time. Not knowing exactly what country to say, Jack just yelled, "Off to the GPF!"

With that command and with a force he'd never experienced before, the lights burst and swallowed Jack into the Magic Map.

Chapter 5:
The Headquarters

When he arrived, Jack found himself
standing all alone in a bitingly cold and
quiet place. There was a steel door with a
screen in the middle facing him, and
another steel door behind. The ceiling
above and walls around him were made
of jagged rock. If Jack had to guess, he
was probably standing in the entranceway
to a building carved into a mountain.

He walked over to the screen on the

steel door. The sign above said: GPF
Identification Lock. He leaned toward the
screen and looked into it. A laser beam
took a picture of his retina. The word
IDENTIFIED flashed across the screen in
green.

Then, an outline of a hand appeared on the screen. Jack placed his right hand over the drawing. His fingers lit up one by one and when the screen had read and recognized all five of his fingerprints, the door to the building unlocked.

Pushing it open, Jack walked through to the other side. Almost as soon as he did, his environment changed. He was standing

in a brightly lit room. People were rushing around carrying papers, while others were chatting away on their phones. Television screens scattered about were showing news about world events.

In front of him was a reception desk. The woman sitting there recognized Jack and smiled.

"Welcome Secret Agent Courage," she

said. "It's so nice to finally meet you in person."

Jack stood, taking it all in. He was at the headquarters of one of the most powerful crime-fighting forces around the world. Even though he was a part of it, he was still temporarily shocked.

"Hi," said Jack, clearing his throat. "I think you're expecting me."

"Yes, we are," she said. "I'll let Director Barter know that you're here." She tapped on an earpiece she was wearing and spoke into a microphone hidden in the cuff of her sleeve.

"Secret Agent Courage is here to see you," she said.

After listening to the reply, she looked up at Jack. "Director Barter will see you now," she said. "Just take the elevator to the second floor. His office will be straight in front of you."

Jack looked past the receptionist. There were two tubelike lifts made of glass that carried passengers to various levels. From Jack's count, there looked to be at least four levels to the GPF HQ.

As Jack made his way to the elevators, he walked by the most amazing looking snowmobile he'd ever seen. It was sitting in the middle of the floor with a sign posted next to it.

GPF SNO-SPEED.
MOST POWERFUL SNOWMOBILE IN THE
WORLD. CAPABLE OF DRIVING ON ICE AND
SNOW AT SPEED OF 200 MPH.
HYDROGEN POWERED. YET ANOTHER GPF
GADGET COMING SOON.

"WOW," thought Jack. "Max would have loved to have seen this." He and his brother, who had gone missing in action while on a GPF assignment, loved fast things.

Tapping the number 2 button on the wall, Jack called for the elevator. When it arrived, the doors opened. A man came out, brushing past Jack.

"Hey," he said, spinning around. "You're Secret Agent Courage!" The man put his hand out to Jack. "Thanks for taking care of that mess with the poachers in Kenya," he said.

Jack was a bit embarrassed. This must be what it felt like to be famous!

"Don't mention it," he said sheepishly, putting his hand out to the man. The man excitedly shook it and then let it go.

"Keep up the good work!" he said, as he patted Jack on the back and walked away.

Jack stepped into the elevator, pushing the right button. It climbed until it reached the second floor.

PING!

The doors opened wide. In front of him was another door. A sign read:

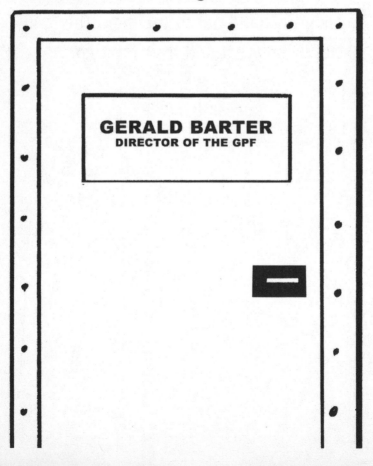

GERALD BARTER
DIRECTOR OF THE GPF

Chapter 6:
The Man in Charge

Jack walked up to the door and tried to relax. He took a deep breath and straightened his clothes. But his stomach was doing flips and his heart was beating fast.

Stop it, he told himself. There's nothing to be nervous about. Think about Director Barter as an ordinary guy. He uses the toilet like everybody else, chews his food like everybody else and probably snores as loud as Dad.

But imagining Gerald Barter as an ordinary person wasn't working for Jack. After all, Mr. Barter was the head of one of the most influential agencies in the world. Most important, he was one of the few people who probably knew something about his brother Max.

Swiftly Jack's thoughts went to his brother. Then a horrible idea struck him. Maybe the director had called him to tell him some terrible news.

Jack gulped and knocked twice.

"Come in," said a voice from the other side.

Turning the handle, Jack pushed the door open. Sitting at a desk at the back of the room was none other than Gerald Barter himself.

"Come in," he said to Jack again. "Close the door behind you."

Jack did as he was told. As he made his way over to the director, he found himself walking on toughened glass. Under the clear flooring was a flattened map of the world. It would have been identical to the Magic Map in Jack's room, if it weren't for the twinkling red lights all over.

"We call that our 'hot zone' map," said the director. "The red lights show us areas of criminal activity." As Jack studied the map, he noticed a few more red lights come up.

"I'm afraid crime never goes away," said the director. "Anyway," he added, pointing to the chair in front of his desk, "why don't you sit so we can talk."

Jack made himself comfortable. The GPF regularly sent pictures of the director out to the press, but they looked nothing like the man seated across from him. This man was handsome, with dark skin and no glasses. The pictures Jack had seen were of a man with lighter skin and thick-rimmed glasses.

Clever, thought Jack. The GPF had been giving the world fake pictures of the director. That way, he'd never be recognized in a crowd, or be the target of a notorious crook.

"The reason I have called you is because we have a serious problem," Barter said.

Jack closed his eyes and hoped there was no bad news about Max.

"Three of our scientists have vanished from here in the Arctic," Barter said. "We need you to locate them and bring them back to safety."

Phew, thought Jack as he opened his eyes. While he wasn't pleased to hear about the scientists, he was relieved there wasn't a terrible development about his brother. Interestingly, the director had said "here in the Arctic," which meant GPF HQ must be somewhere near the North Pole. It would explain why he was so cold when he first arrived.

"Were these the scientists studying global warming?" asked Jack.

The director nodded in agreement. He seemed pleased that Jack was on top of the latest GPF news.

"Here they are," said Barter, showing

Jack a collection of photos taken of the team. "Study their faces so you can recognize them later. They checked in yesterday morning before they set off," he explained. "They didn't tell us where they were going; only that it was unchartered territory. Unfortunately, we haven't heard from them since."

"Maybe they're still at work," said Jack. "Perhaps they decided to camp out and return later than expected."

"That's not possible," said Barter. "They're under strict instructions to report back to the hut. After all, nighttime temperatures are extremely low and there are hungry polar bears roaming about."

"I'm assuming they would have traveled by snowmobile," said Jack. "What about their radios?" All GPF snowmobiles were equipped with sophisticated communication and navigation equipment.

"We're getting nothing but static," said Barter. "Someone or something has disabled their systems."

The whole thing did seem strange to Jack. How could a team of scientists completely vanish? There was no way a single polar bear could have brought down three adults. Maybe, thought Jack, they'd fallen through the ice.

"Can you show me where their warming

hut was located?" asked Jack. He figured it would be a good place to start looking for clues.

"Here," said the director, pointing to a map on his desk. His finger was showing an area 150 miles away.

"Then that's where I'll begin," said Jack. Before he got up, Jack thought of another question. "If you don't mind me asking, why didn't you send somebody else—somebody based here at the GPF HQ?"

"Because," said the director with a smile, "I needed my best agent for this job. I don't need to tell you how critical this mission is. The work of these scientists could have a major impact on our lives here on Earth."

Jack agreed. Aside from finding his brother, he couldn't think of a bigger mission. He wanted to ask Director Barter something about Max. As he opened his mouth, the director chimed in.

"Look," he said, almost reading Jack's mind. "I know this thing with your brother has been difficult. We're doing our best to try and locate him. As soon as we do," he added, "we'll let you know."

Jack acted relieved, but something was still nagging at him. The tone of the director's voice and his body language hinted that he knew something more. But Jack couldn't very well challenge him without any solid evidence. Not here. Not now.

"I'll do my best to find the scientists," said Jack, focusing on the mission at hand.

"Thank you," said the director. "Why don't you take the elevator to the ground level. Mr. Davidson has something for you."

Mr. Davidson was the GPF's technology wizard. He'd single-handedly designed and built nearly every gadget in the GPF arsenal. He'd been working for the GPF ever since it began. The Hypno-Disc, the Torpedo, the Flyboard and the Melting Ink Pen were just some of his fantastic creations.

Jack took the map from the director's desk and rushed to the door. He was excited—it wasn't every day an agent got to meet the man responsible for some of the greatest GPF gadgets of all time.

Waving goodbye to the director, Jack stepped back into the hallway. He took the lift to the ground level. When he got there, he found himself staring at another steel door. On it was another sign that said: SPEAK. Jack said "hello," and when the door recognized his voice, it slid open.

Chapter 7:
The Tech Guy

"Welcome, Secret Agent Courage!" boomed a voice.

It was Mr. Davidson, and he was standing in the middle of an underground warehouse. Jack guessed the lanky man was sixty years old, but given how animated he was he could have been decades younger.

"It's so nice to meet you," he said, quickly approaching. He grabbed Jack's

hand and shook it furiously. After he was
finished, Jack put his throbbing hand in
his pocket.

"This is where it all happens!" Mr.
Davidson said, spinning around on his
heels. He was showing Jack one of the
biggest collections of super spy gadgets
in the world.

Mr. Davidson led Jack around the room by the elbow. They passed by hundreds of high-tech gadgets, many that Jack recognized and many more that he didn't.

"Why don't we come over here," said Mr. Davidson, leading Jack to a stepladder in the middle of the room. "I want to show you something," he added.

They climbed the steps together until

the ladder stopped at the edge of a platform. On the platform was something large underneath a beige tarpaulin.

"When Director Barter told me what you were up to, I decided to put a rush on this." With one stroke of the hand Mr. Davidson pulled off the tarpaulin, unveiling the hidden object.

Jack stared at none other than the GPF Sno-Speed—the high-tech snowmobile he'd seen in the reception area.

"You're joking," said Jack, who couldn't believe his luck. "You mean I get to ride this thing? Wow!"

"Yep!" said Mr. Davidson. "Consider yourself the 'test' agent."

Mr. Davidson showed Jack around the vehicle and how to activate its hydrogen-powered engine. He then demonstrated how several of its features worked. At the front was a satellite navigation screen, as well as a spotlight for seeing things in the dark. Tucked away into a door on the side was a sharp, serrated knife. On the dash was a "silencer" button that would turn the noise of the engine completely off.

Lastly, and most impressive, Mr. Davidson told Jack how the "mental telepathy" feature worked. If Jack was lost or in trouble, all he had to do was call the vehicle with his mind. The Sno-Speed would start up and find him wherever he was.

"Impressive," Jack said to Mr. Davidson, although he secretly doubted something like that would actually work.

"And I have something else for you," Mr. Davidson said, dashing down the ladder and to a closet at the back of the warehouse. When he returned, he was carrying a thin yellow parka.

"Wear this," he said. "It will help keep you warm. Those Arctic winds are freezing."

Jack had read about the GPF's Polar Parka. It was made of a special fabric that reacted to outside temperature. The colder it got outside, the warmer it got on the inside. What was also great about the Polar Parka was that it glowed in the dark. So if an agent was lost in a snowstorm or at night, they would be easier to find.

"Thanks," said Jack, slipping on the Polar Parka under his Book Bag and climbing onto the Sno-Speed.

"How do I look?" Jack asked.

"Super!" replied Mr. Davidson. "But you need a helmet."

"Right," said Jack, who pulled his Noggin Mold out of his Book Bag.

Once the flexible plastic had hardened to Jack's head, Mr. Davidson rushed down the steps and over to a big green button on the opposite wall. He punched it, opening another sliding door. A cold blast of wind and snow flurries flew in.

"Now be careful," he warned. "I don't want to be reading about you getting into trouble in the next edition of the GPF News!"

"Don't worry," said Jack. "I'll try and make sure that doesn't happen."

He started the engine and positioned

the nose of the snowmobile over the ramp below. With a twist of the accelerator, the Sno-Speed flew through the warehouse and out into the snow.

Chapter 8:
The Hut

Almost as soon as Jack was outside in the
daylight, he turned around to wave to Mr.
Davidson. But there was nothing behind
him but a mountain covered in snow. There
was no sign of the door he'd come through,
nor any hint of the GPF headquarters
inside. He wondered whether he'd dreamed
the whole thing, but after looking at his
Polar Parka and Sno-Speed he knew what
had happened was real.

Jack pulled out the map that Gerald Barter had given him. He looked to the coordinates of the warming hut. Programming them into the navigation screen on the Sno-Speed, Jack put his paper map away. He sat for a moment and looked around. The Arctic was absolutely stunning. It was the most beautiful place Jack had ever seen.

It was early spring, which meant after months of being barely above the horizon, the sun was back in the sky. Now that it was shining, the ground was a glittering white and the sky a crystal blue. The ice and snow went on for miles.

After traveling for a while, he saw a small building up ahead. According to his navigation device, this was the scientists' warming hut. Jack pulled up alongside the weatherproof building, and began to look for clues.

But there was nothing to be found. There was a thermometer, a few solar

panels on the roof, an outhouse and an empty tool box. There weren't any tracks from the team's snowmobiles or signs of a struggle with a polar bear. Whatever had happened to them must have happened after they left. But where did they go? Because it looked like it had recently snowed, Jack couldn't tell which direction they had gone.

Maybe, Jack reckoned, searching inside would give him an idea. Using his Magic Key Maker, Jack unlocked the door and stepped inside.

The hut was one large room. In front of him were three beds, and to his right was a small kitchen. To his left was a lounge area with a simple communication system. In the center of the room was an aluminum table. The table had a sheet of paper on top. Jack walked over and studied it carefully.

But this wasn't just any piece of paper. It was a map. Colored lines were drawn from an *X* in the middle outward. Jack figured the *X* was the location of the warming hut. The lines marked the routes the scientists had traveled. At the end of each line was a dot, and next to each dot was a handwritten date.

If Jack could find a dot with yesterday's

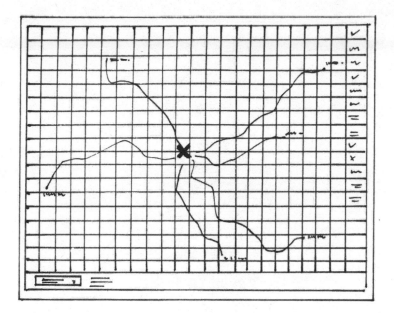

date, he could trace the path the scientists had taken. Spying a blue dot with the right date, Jack made a note of the coordinates. He rushed out of the hut, jumped on his Sno-Speed and programmed the details of his next destination.

"Don't worry," said Jack out loud. "I'm coming to rescue you." And then he sped off.

Chapter 9:
The Find

Jack and his Sno-Speed traveled at a
blistering pace over the Arctic ice. The
screen on the Sno-Speed not only told
him how fast he was going (90 mph) but
also whether there was ice or land or a
combination of both below. As he
traveled, the ice-covered land changed to
ice alone. Jack was now speeding along
on top of the frozen Arctic Sea.

In the distance, he could see a polar

bear—one of the most feared killers of the Arctic. Male polar bears could weigh up to around 1,540 pounds and grow as long as a one-story building. They mostly preyed on seals, but Jack knew if they were desperate they'd pretty much eat anything. As he sat on his Sno-Speed, Jack was relieved that he was far away. The last thing he wanted was to be within striking distance of a creature like that.

Further ahead, he could see something in the glistening snow. It looked like a trio of snowmobiles. Jack increased his speed and hurried along.

When he got there, he recognized them as the wrecked snowmobiles of the missing scientists. No wonder Director Barter wasn't able to get a signal, thought Jack. Their communication systems were pretty bashed up. But where was the team?

Jack walked around the vehicles looking for clues. In front of them, he spied some footprints. Following them as they traveled north, he noticed they doubled back on themselves. Somewhere in the mess of footprints, Jack noticed something pink glistening in the snow. He knelt down to get a better look. It resembled a fine pink dust.

Not sure what it was or whether to

touch it, Jack pulled out his Poison Tracker device. The GPF's Poison Tracker was an all-in-one kit that could analyze any substance (liquid or dry) and tell an agent whether to beware. If the glass on the vial turned red it meant the substance was deadly. Yellow meant dangerous. Green meant it was harmless.

Slipping on his protective gloves, Jack scooped up the dust with a small spoon and tapped it into a glass vial. He put the top on and shook it hard. Within seconds, the vial turned yellow. DANGEROUS.

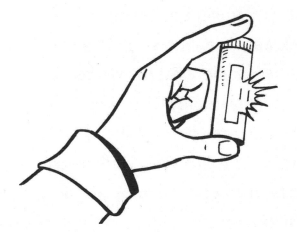

Jack snapped off his gloves and put them away. The scientists seemed to have been drugged, but with what? Maybe it was a paralyzing potion that had crippled their muscles. Or, maybe it was a dozing dust. Either way, Jack had to figure out where they were—and fast.

He looked to the ground again. Traveling from where he stood were snowmobile tracks different than those made by GPF vehicles. He followed the marks with his eyes, and saw that they led to some huts in the distance. Jack hurried back to his Sno-Speed.

If Jack was right, the scientists had been drugged and carted away to those buildings. Maybe they'd seen something they shouldn't have. Maybe they were captured because of their work. Maybe they were just in the wrong place at the wrong time.

But those possible reasons didn't really matter. What mattered to Jack was that innocent people were being held hostage. Those poor scientists were probably dazed, cold and hungry.

It was these thoughts that filled Jack's mind. With the faces of the scientists burned on his brain, Jack pushed the silencer button on the Sno-Speed's engine and set off. The wind against Jack's face felt even colder now. In the beautiful but harsh Arctic, there was never a moment to waste.

Chapter 10:
The Tipped Cane

As Jack approached the buildings, he counted three huts. The one in front was large, while the other two were much smaller. Surrounding the back was a fence made of barrels. Jack navigated the Sno-Speed toward it and stopped the engine.

Climbing off the vehicle, he crouched down and scurried along the fence. Out of nowhere, Jack heard two men talking. He dropped to the ice and held his breath.

"What should we do?" said one voice.

"Let's lay some more tarp," said the
other.

Jack risked a peek over the barrels. The
two men were wearing black helmets with
flames on the sides. Although their visors
were lifted, Jack couldn't see much of
their faces.

Heading to one of the smaller huts, the men flung open the doors. Jack could see large rolls of black tarpaulin stacked high inside. The men clambered to the top of the pile and rolled two down. They then lugged them through the snow and attached them to their snowmobiles.

"Will those geeks be OK without us?" asked one, climbing onto his vehicle.

"Yeah," said the other, doing the same. "They're not going anywhere."

They started their snowmobiles and took off. Jack wasn't sure what they were doing with that tarp, but he knew one thing—these were the guys who had snatched the scientists. And because of what they'd said, he knew the team was inside one of the huts.

Running along the fence, Jack headed to the main building. The front door was locked, so he used his Magic Key Maker.

After pushing this thin piece of plastic into the keyhole, it melted and then hardened to form a perfect key. Jack turned the lock and the door popped open. As soon as he was inside, he began looking around. The rooms were separated by hanging sheets of weather-proof material. It was like a mega-sized family tent, the kind Jack's family took on camping holidays to the New Forest.

Dashing from one room to the next,

Jack pushed the sheets as he went. In one of the rooms, he saw an open laptop. On the screen was a draft of an e-mail waiting to be sent. Jack read it carefully. It was addressed to an ag@woandg.com.

Project Black Arctic is proceeding well. Only a few more weeks and Phase I will be complete.
Regards,
G. R. Slick

Except for the GPF's global warming research, Jack wasn't aware of any other legal projects going on in the Arctic. He wondered what the phrase "Black Arctic" meant, and which of the two men was G. R. Slick.

He was about to re-read the e-mail when a male voice shouted at him from behind. "What are you doing in my office?"

Startled, Jack turned around to see someone altogether different from the two men he'd seen before. This man was tall with greasy black hair, and a face that hadn't been shaved in days. His two front teeth stuck out like a beaver's, and his feet were the length of two small boats. Since the man referred to the area as his office, Jack figured he was G. R. Slick.

"Answer me!" he shouted at Jack. "What the devil are you doing reading my personal e-mails?"

From behind, the man pulled out a wooden cane. He whacked Jack's body with it as hard as he could.

"Arrgh!" Jack yelled in agony, and collapsed to the floor.

As the pain wore off, Jack stood up to face Mr. Slick. When he did, Mr. Slick put the tip of the cane between his eyes. At its tip was a sharp metal point. Jack knew if he moved, Mr. Slick could blind him with one poke.

"Now," said Mr. Slick, "I'll ask you one more time." He leaned in further. "What are you doing snooping around?"

Just then, Jack heard footsteps. The two men he'd seen outside had come back.

"What's the matter, boss?" they asked.

They were breathing heavily, as if they'd been running.

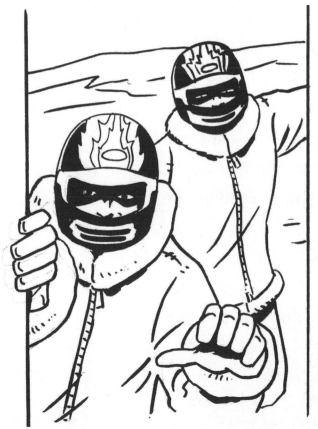

Jack thought carefully about what to do next. He decided the best thing to do was to trick Mr. Slick into keeping him alive.

"My name is Jack Jones," he said. "And I work for the Worldwide Animal Group. We're researching polar bears in the Arctic. You know," he added quickly, "tracking their moves and documenting how they take care of their young."

Mr. Slick and his men were glaring at him but listening. Jack carried on.

"I saw these huts," he explained, "and I thought perhaps you were part of my group. The Worldwide Animal Group said they were sending other researchers out here. So I came in to have a look."

Jack waited for a response. Mr. Slick started to laugh, soon joined by the other two men. But this wasn't a funny ha-ha kind of laugh. It was much more sinister than that.

"You expect me to believe that?" cackled Mr. Slick. "You know what I think," he said, turning to his men. "I think this punk has come looking for his friends. Why don't we put him with the others?"

With Mr. Slick's cane still pointed between Jack's eyes, one of his men lifted a long tube and pumped a lever underneath. Mr. Slick backed away. The other two men put their visors down.

Within moments, a fine pink dust was released into the air around Jack's nose. He frantically tried to cover his nostrils, but it was too late. The dangerous dust had entered his body.

"You're going to regret messing with me," said Mr. Slick.

The next thing Jack knew, his body felt heavy. Within seconds everything went black.

"Pick him up," snarled Mr. Slick, as he pointed to Jack's limp body. "And keep your eyes out for more trespassers," he growled. "It seems as though everybody and their grandmother is in the Arctic today."

With that, Mr. Slick twirled on the point of his cane. He left the hut and his men to do what they were ordered. They scraped Jack's body off the floor and carried him away.

Chapter 11:
The Reason

Jack wasn't sure how long he'd been drugged, but when he finally came to it felt like an eternity. His body was stiff and achey and he could barely open his eyes. In the background, he could hear voices.

"Is that who I think it is?" said one.

"I think so," said another.

"Do you think he's come here to help?" asked a third.

Jack found himself lying sideways on

the floor. Staring at him from across the way were three people: one woman and two men. Jack recognized their faces from the pictures in Director Barter's office. They were the missing scientists. Now all he had to do was get himself off of the floor, call the GPF and get rid of those nasty men for good.

But Jack couldn't move. His wrists and feet were tied together. There was no way he could reach his Watch Phone.

"It won't work," said one of the
scientists. "They're pretty good at tying
people up." With their eyes, they
motioned to Jack to show that they too
had been tied up.

"My name is Elsa," said the woman
scientist.

"I'm Ted," said one of the men.

"And I'm Jordan," said the last.

Jack began to introduce himself too, but
Elsa interrupted. "We know who you are,"
she said.

Again, Jack was a bit embarrassed. This was the second time in a short while that someone had recognized him for his secret agent skills and success rate.

"So," said Jack. "Tell me what happened."

Ted started first. "We came out this way," he said, "to measure the thickness of the ice. As we were getting our gear together, Jordan noticed these huts."

"So we decided to check them out," added Jordan, "and these goons came out of nowhere. They sprayed us with dust, and that's how we ended up here."

"Did you see anyone or anything else?" asked Jack.

"There was a big explosion," said Elsa.

"What kind of explosion?" asked Jack.

"The kind you get with dynamite," said Ted. "It blew up large chunks of the ice."

Jack thought about Mr. Slick's e-mail.

He wondered if blowing up bits of Arctic ice was part of this "Black Arctic" project. He wondered what else was part of his plan.

"In one of the smaller huts," said Jack, "I saw loads of rolled-up black tarp. Any idea what that could be about?"

They all thought for a moment, and then Elsa, the female scientist, gasped.

"What's the matter?" asked Jack.

"Well," she said. "It's only an idea. But it makes sense."

Jack and the men listened as she spoke.

"The Arctic," Elsa said, "is heating up more than any place on Earth. There's less white ice available to reflect the sun's energy back. Since there is less ice and more dark water, the exposed water is making the melting worse."

The men nodded in agreement and all three looked at Jack.

"According to our work here this spring," she added, "Ted, Jordan and I are estimating that the Arctic may lose all of its ice by 2030. That is, unless we try to stop global warming. If I'm right," she added, "these men are trying to hurry it up."

"By breaking up the ice and using the black tarp to absorb more heat?" asked Jack.

Elsa nodded.

"But why would they want to do that?" yelled Jordan in frustration. "They must be nuts! Our planet is already in crisis. Don't they know it would make matters worse?"

"Maybe they do, and maybe they don't," said Jack. "The important thing is that we have to stop them."

Jack wondered why they were doing all

of this, and then he remembered the e-mail he'd seen. Mr. Slick had written to an ag@woandg.com. If Jack could figure out who that was, it might help him answer the "why."

Chapter 12:
The Evil Plan

Just then, the door banged open.

BLAM!

A cold rush of air swept in. It was Mr. Slick and his men. Jack looked desperately at his Watch Phone. If only he could reach the key pad with the fingers on his right hand.

Mr. Slick noticed Jack glancing at his wrist. "What have we here?" he said, leaning down to Jack's level. "Is that one

of those silly radio devices?"
Mr. Slick's bony fingers
pried the gadget off
Jack's wrist. Standing
up with it in his
hand, he tilted it
and then
looked at its
underside.

"Yes," he said to his men. "I think we
should definitely get rid of this."

Then he threw the gadget to the
ground, lifted his cane and with one
thrust of its metal spike split it in two.

"There," he said, kicking the pieces
across the floor. "That should stop you
from calling for help."

As Jack sat in momentary shock, he realized Mr. Slick wasn't finished yet. His evil eyes were fixed on Jack.

"I've heard there's some polar bear activity in this area," he carried on. "And since you were part of the—what did you call it—Worldwide Animal Group," he said, "I thought you'd like to see one up close. Lucky you!"

Jack narrowed his eyes back to Mr. Slick. He didn't like the sound of him or his plan. But at this point, Jack didn't have any choice but to go along. He'd have to look for another opportunity to escape.

"Drag them out!" ordered Mr. Slick.

Mr. Slick's henchmen pulled Elsa, Ted and Jordan from their seats and out of the door. Although they shouted for help as best as they could, their cries were swallowed up by the icy wilderness.

Then the men came back for Jack. They grabbed him by the arms and dragged him outside. There was a trailer attached to one of the snowmobiles. Forcing all four of them onto it, the bad guys climbed on top of their snowmobiles.

As they traveled south, Jack wondered what Mr. Slick was planning. Was he going to leave them out there alone? Or was he planning something else?

Hoping it was the former, Jack thought through his options. Not too far away, he saw a large polar bear on the horizon. Mr. Slick looked at Jack, baring his horrible yellow teeth.

"I'm going to get you!" Jack snarled at Mr. Slick.

Laughing, Mr. Slick ordered his goons to keep moving ahead. When they were within 100 yards of the bear, the men slowed down. Mr. Slick spoke to Jack and the scientists.

"This is as far as we're going," he said. "I personally don't want to be within a whiff of that bear. We'll be leaving you here to fend for yourselves. I'm sure it will come and say hello in no time!"

Mr. Slick's men lugged the scientists and Jack out of the trailer. They tossed the four of them onto the snow.

"Toodles," said Mr. Slick. "Happy eating!"

Then Mr. Slick and his men left them alone on the ice.

Chapter 13:
The Savior

"We have to get out of here!" cried Elsa. "That bear's going to smell us!"

Almost as soon as she said that, Jack saw the bear lift its nose in the air. It had done what Mr. Slick predicted, it had gotten a whiff of their scent and was making its way over.

"Hurry!" yelled Ted. Everyone was yanking at their ties, trying to wriggle free.

"Don't worry," said Jack. "I have a plan."

He closed his eyes and concentrated hard.
Jack was trying to call his Sno-Speed.

When Mr. Davidson showed Jack
around the Sno-Speed, he had told him
about its "mental telepathy" feature—
the ability to read an agent's mind.
All Jack had to do was think very hard
and the Sno-Speed would come to get
him. Thanks to the transponder Jack
wore on his body, it would also know
where to go.

"It's coming!" shouted Jordan.
Jack opened his eyes. Unfortunately,
Jordan wasn't talking about the Sno-
Speed. He was talking about the bear.
The noise and their scent had drawn it to
them. It was now running toward them—
at a frightening rate.

Desperately the foursome rolled to their
sides and got to their feet. They were
hopping as best as they could in an
attempt to get away.

But Jack and the scientists knew it was no use. Polar bears could run at 25 miles per hour. Given its current speed and the short distance between them, Jack figured it would arrive within seconds.

Just then, Jack saw a yellow blur out of the corner of his eye. He looked to his right. There was the Sno-Speed! Mr. Davidson had come up trumps again with another life-saving gadget.

On seeing the Sno-Speed, the bear stopped in its tracks. Confused and wondering what this strange object was, the bear turned and loped off in the other direction.

The Sno-Speed glided in front of Jack. Jack bent down and twisted himself, so that his wrists were up against its side. He pushed a button that released a small, jagged knife from the side compartment. Grabbing onto it with his fingers, he sawed through the rope on his wrists. He then cut himself free at the feet. One by one he released the scientists too.

"So," said Jordan, "what's next?" Jack climbed on top of the Sno-Speed and turned on the main screen. He sent an e-mail to Director Barter telling him what had happened, and calling for reinforcements. Unfortunately, Jack knew that it would still take them a while to get there.

Just then, another explosion could be heard. Jack and the scientists saw huge chunks of ice fly into the air and back onto the ground.

"Those guys have to be stopped—and now," said Jack. "Unfortunately, I have to do this myself."

The scientists knew that GPF agents worked alone, or with other people so long as they wouldn't get in the way. There were three adults in addition to Jack. There was no way he could take all of them along.

Reaching into his Book Bag, Jack pulled out a small disc made out of nylon. This was the GPF's Base Camp. When Jack threw it to the ground, it fanned open into a large weatherproof tent. He rummaged around his Book Bag and pulled out the GPF's Portable Tea Makers. They may not be strictly life-saving gadgets, but these collapsible cups containing tea bags would be a comfort to the scientists stuck in the cold. The last thing he gave them was a bottle of water.

"Just pour that into those cups and

you'll be fine," said Jack, climbing back
onto his Sno-Speed. Jack knew the cups
contained a thermostat that would heat
the water themselves. "Thanks, Jack,"
said Elsa. "We know you can do it."

"You're the best," said Ted, giving Jack
a high-five.

"No worries," said Jack. "I'll stop these guys."

He waved goodbye to the scientists, just as another bomb went off in the distance.

KABOOM!

Chapter 14:
The Hole in the Ice

Finding Mr. Slick and his henchmen would
be easy, thought Jack. He'd just have to
follow the exploding ice. As he traveled,
Jack spied large sheets of black tarp
covering the ground. Not too far away
were Mr. Slick and one of his men. They
were busy looking at something on the
ground. Their backs were to Jack, so it
was a perfect time to strike.

With the silencer still on the Sno-Speed,

Jack aimed it straight for them. He stood up to give himself leverage and pulled his Net Tosser out of his Book Bag. Just as he was about to throw it over the crooks, something hit him from behind.

SMACK!

Jack's body was hurled over the handle-bars and onto the snow. As he lay there stunned, he saw another snowmobile drive by. On it was the second of Mr. Slick's men. He laughed as he skidded past Jack.

Quickly Jack started to run. He still had the Net Tosser in his hands. Sprinting as fast as he could, he flung the gadget in Mr. Slick's direction. But Mr. Slick hobbled out of the way. It sailed past him and fell on the dusty snow.

Drat, thought Jack. He was going to have to think of something else. By now, Mr. Slick and his men had positioned themselves together as a trio, daring Jack to come their way.

Past them Jack saw an enormous hole in the ice. It must have been what Mr. Slick was looking at earlier. Figuring they'd caused it by that recent explosion, Jack had an idea of what to do next.

He pulled an oval-shaped plastic board out of his Book Bag. This was the GPF's Sno-Sled—the fastest way to slide in the snow. Sensing Jack was up to something, Mr. Slick and his men tried to protect themselves. Mr. Slick lifted his metal-tipped cane. One of his goons had that long tube; the other pulled out some sort of spiked ball on a rope.

But they weren't expecting what happened next. Jack picked up speed and sat in the middle of the Sno-Sled. As it accelerated, he held onto the handles.

Like a bowling ball, he crashed into the men's feet and sent them sailing backward into the hole in the ice.

SPLASH!

Jack and his Sno-Sled stopped short of the edge. Knowing the men could freeze in minutes, he had to get them out as fast as he could. He needed to rescue them, or he'd never figure out what the Black Arctic project was all about.

Giving the men his hand, he pulled them out one at a time. Just as he expected, Mr. Slick and his men were too cold to fight back. As he hauled them up onto the ice, Jack put some GPF handcuffs around their wrists. Then he put some foil blankets on the men to keep them warm.

Once he'd gotten them settled, Jack turned to Mr. Slick.

"Who are you working for?" he demanded.

Mr. Slick paused for a second then looked at Jack. Jack could tell in his eyes he was exhausted. After that dip in the frozen water, he looked like he'd aged at least ten years.

"Oh, what the heck, I'm getting too old for this stuff. Plus," he added, "I'm not getting paid enough. We were hired by Anton Gustavson."

Jack couldn't believe what he was hearing. Anton Gustavson was the president of the Wellem Oil and Gas Company.

"What did he want you to do?" asked Jack.

"Mr. Gustavson hired us to destroy the ice," Slick explained. "That way, he could access the oil easier, and use the Northwest Passage to ship it out."

Now Jack realized what the "black" meant in Black Arctic. The Arctic was seen by many as the last frontier when it came to precious oil. Billions of barrels' worth were thought to be trapped under the

Arctic sea. But drilling companies couldn't get to it easily if the ice was on the top and in the way. Blowing it up and melting it with that black tarp would make things easier. Plus, in accelerating the melt, the Northwest Passage (a normally frozen sea channel) would be available for ships to carry the oil out and sell it to the rest of the world. They had been attempting to speed up global warming for selfish, greedy needs—and Jack had stopped them in the nick of time.

Just then, Jack heard a comforting noise in the distance. It was the sound of several snowmobiles. The GPF backup troops had finally arrived.

Chapter 15:
The Director

One of the lead snowmobiles came up to Jack. An adult driver got off and introduced himself to Jack. He said his name was Pablo and he worked for Director Barter.

"Well," he said. "It looks like you've solved another crime."

"Yep," said Jack. "These criminals are ready for taking away. We also need to arrest Mr. Anton Gustavson, since he's the one who hired these men to destroy the ice."

"Why would he want to do that?" asked Pablo.

"Because he is a greedy man, who wants more oil," said Jack.

"What about the scientists?" Pablo said. "Are they all right?"

"They're OK now," said Jack. "They were just in the wrong place at the wrong time."

Jack gave Pablo the coordinates of the GPF Base Camp. He knew the scientists would be in good hands, and thanks to Jack would publish their findings as soon as they could.

"One more thing," said Jack. "We need to get rid of all this black tarp on the ice."

"Will do," said Pablo. "Director Barter is proud of you. He wants to speak to you now."

Pablo handed over a small videophone, and then stepped away. On the screen was a man with light skin and thick-rimmed specs. Jack was confused. This wasn't the man he'd met in the director's office.

"Great job, Secret Agent Courage," he said. "I knew you could do it."

"Thanks," said Jack. "So which one of you is the real director?"

"I'm afraid that's a secret that I can never reveal," the man said, before signing off with a smile.

Pablo came up to Jack. "I notice you aren't wearing your Watch Phone," he said.

"Yeah," said Jack, rubbing his wrist, "Mr. Slick broke it in two."

"Take this one," said Pablo, handing Jack a new Watch Phone.

As Jack thanked Pablo and strapped the watch onto his wrist, he looked over at Mr. Slick. His beaver teeth were still chattering, but he would survive. He and his men were about to be sent  to an international prison. Crimes this big against the environment affected all countries. Mr. Gustavson, Mr. Slick and his gang were definitely going away for a long time.

Once the commotion had died down, Jack tapped into his new Watch Phone. He called up a map of the world and pulled up the country of Great Britain.

There were no secrets among fellow GPF members. In front of everyone, he waited until a light shined brightly. When he was ready, he yelled "Off to England!"

Chapter 16:
The Last Word

When Jack arrived home the first thing he did was head to his computer, sign on and pull up his report on global warming. Although he'd written most of it, there was still some finishing up to do.

Tapping as furiously as he could, he added:

Many people think global warming doesn't exist. Or, that if it does, it will only give us sunnier weather. The truth is global warming is one of the biggest threats to humankind. Heating up the world, even by a few degrees, can change our weather and threaten everything that lives on Earth. Many animals, like the polar bear, may even die out in the next thirty years. That's why we have to do what we can to make a difference.

The single biggest thing that we can do is to cut down on the electricity we use. Most people don't know it, but electricity is made by burning coal. If we use less electricity, we burn less carbon dioxide. That means we should turn out the lights when we leave a room, and the power strips that run our computers. Another easy thing is to get our parents to change a light bulb.

If everyone in the country changed just one light bulb to one that says "CFL," it would be like taking one million cars off the road.

A normal household has at least fifteen to thirty light bulbs! Imagine if every kid nagged their parents to change them all; we really could save the world. Another thing we can do is use our bikes, skateboards and feet instead of cars to get around.

Global warming doesn't have to be scary. There are lots of villains out there who'd like it to succeed. But if we pull together, we can stop them and global warming altogether.

Jack pressed the "print" button and watched as his report came out. Exhausted from his trip, he switched the electrical power strip linked to his computer to "off" and changed into his pajamas. He crawled into bed and turned his nightlight off.

As he lay there letting his body sink into the mattress, he thought about the majesty of the Arctic. Knowing he'd rid that beautiful place of Mr. Slick and his goons made Jack smile with pride.

Tomorrow Jack would likely be off on another mission. He wondered where he was off to, and what kind of nasty villain he'd face. With dreams of exciting adventures ahead, Jack closed his eyes and drifted off to sleep.